# LONE WOLF

## ALAN GIBBONS AND ROBBIE GIBBONS

Illustrated by

**Matt Timson**

# Chapter 1

Danny quickened his pace. It was getting dark. He glanced at his watch. 6:30 p.m. He was late. He turned a corner and passed a "MISSING" poster taped to a lamppost, a reminder of why Mum wanted him home early. Ten people had disappeared in the last month. Mum had even put pepper spray in his backpack. That was Mum, always worrying.

Her voice echoed in his head. "Make sure you're back by six."

He checked his watch again. 6:40. Uh-oh. Better take the short-cut, he thought.

Big mistake.

Jay Carver and his gang were at their usual spot by the shops. Their eyes locked on Danny. He remembered why he usually took the long way round. He tried to walk past but they blocked his path.

"Where do you think you're going?" Carver said. He didn't wait for an answer.

The punch shook Danny's jaw. His face hit the pavement with a crack. He tasted blood. Carver's pack of hyenas was pointing, laughing. Danny's vision blurred as tears burned at the corners of his eyes. The shame stung worse than the pain. He made a run for it, heading for the line of trees at the roadside.

"Get him!" Carver shouted.

# Chapter 2

Danny knew they were on his tail, but didn't dare look back in case he tripped. He ran deeper into the woods. Twigs and dry leaves crunched under his trainers. When he thought he'd run a safe distance, he skidded to a stop and pressed his back to a tree trunk. He panted for breath. His ears prickled. Silence.

He peered over his shoulder. All he saw were the naked trees stretching out until they sunk into the fog. He'd lost Carver and the gang, but he couldn't shake off the feeling he was being watched.

The darkness swallowed him. The trees hissed whispers and warnings.

A thrash of branches made his head snap round.

"Who's there?" he asked. The answer was a low growl.

He saw it in flashes: a shadow of prickly fur, the gleam of teeth. The sight of it snatched the breath from Danny's lungs. He knew what the creature was. He thought they had died out in Britain hundreds of years ago, but there was no doubt about it.

He was looking into the yellow eyes of a wolf.

The beast prowled silently towards him. The huge muscles of its back and shoulders shifted beneath its fur.

s

a

sk

D

had

It hiss

A pa

chance

street lig

Thin bra

his heart f

8

# Chapter 3

When Danny finally got home, Mum went mental. He stood sheepishly in the hall, shifting his weight from one foot to the other. When she asked how he had hurt his arm so badly, he didn't tell her about the wolf. It would have sounded like the lamest excuse ever: *Sorry I was late, Mum, I got attacked by a wolf.* Yeah, right.

"I was running because I was late. I wasn't looking where I was going." He could feel her eyes burrowing into him. After a pause he added, "Sorry."

"I'll get the disinfectant," Mum sighed, and went off to the kitchen.

.eaned himself up in the bathroom.

_d his elbows on the sink and massaged

_mples. He could feel a headache coming on.

_ne pain throbbed. It made it hard to concentrate.
He ran the tap and splashed cool water over his
face. When he looked into the mirror, he frowned.
A bruise was coming up where Carver had hit him.
It covered half of his face.

Danny took a deep breath. He could have
told Mum about being jumped by Carver – it
would have explained why he was late and how
he cut his arm – but he said nothing. He was
embarrassed. He remembered the mocking faces,
the laughter. Danny reddened. His fists clenched
until his nails bit half-moon shapes into his palms.

Next time he wouldn't run. Next time he would
stay and fight, even if it meant losing.

# Chapter 4

Danny noticed something: a hair that looked out of place. He gave it a tug and it came out with a little pinch of pain. It was long and wiry, metallic grey. Weird. He shrugged and flicked the hair into the bin, but when he looked back there was another one in its place, long and grey just like the first. *Very* weird.

He spotted another one, and another. They seemed to be appearing right in front of his eyes. Danny's heart pounded. He locked himself in the bathroom. When he looked in the mirror again, hairs were already bursting from his face. They punched through his skin like needles. He groaned in agony.

There was a tap on the door. "You okay?" Mum asked.

Danny could smell her on the other side of the doorway. Not her perfume, but *her*. It was the smell of the blood rushing through her veins. It made him feel hungry. *What's happening to me?*

"Fine," he croaked, struggling to control the pain.

Mum made a little noise of understanding. "Use the air freshener when you're done."

Danny waited until her footsteps padded away. When he was sure she was gone, he ran down the stairs and straight out of the door.

The pain got worse as he staggered down the street. He could feel his muscles expanding, his bones bending into new shapes. He heard the rip of his clothes shredding to pieces. He tried to scream, but instead what escaped from his throat was a long howl that echoed around the quiet streets. When he dragged himself up to a puddle to check his reflection, he shrank back: the matted fur, the long muzzle, the dagger-like claws.

Wolf.

# Chapter 5

Something was building inside him. It pulled at his stomach. Hunger. Danny knew it was the hunger for blood.

He tried to fight it, but it was no use. The animal was in control.

Danny followed the nearest scent to the edge of the woods. A rabbit was nibbling on some leafy weeds. It bolted when he came close. It was fast, but not fast enough. He caught it in his jaws and shook it from side to side. When it was dead he ate the remains whole, grinding the bones to dust with his teeth.

In half an hour he had caught two more rabbits and a squirrel. He still wasn't full, not even close. There was another scent on the wind. It was stronger, harder to resist. Human blood.

The human in Danny screamed *no*, but the wolf snarled it away.

He raced off after the smell. His paws pounded on the pavement. He moved so fast that the streets whipped past in a blur.

He found his prey down a quiet side street, a man in a suit. He slowed and crept in the shadows. The man's shoulders stiffened. Danny knew the feeling, the feeling that you're being watched.

The man turned. His eyes widened. His briefcase clattered to the floor and littered the street with paper, but he didn't run. Shock kept his feet planted. Danny lunged and pinned him to the ground.

Just as he was about to clamp his jaws around his victim's neck, their eyes met. Danny saw the fear in them, the hopelessness. In their tear-filled sheen he saw his own. They were the glowing, yellow eyes of a killer.

He stopped. The trance was broken. It was as if he had just woken from a deep sleep. He could feel himself changing. His muscles deflated. His claws disappeared under his fingernails. His hairs pulled back into his skin.

"I'm sorry," he said. His voice was a growl, still half wolf.

He ran off into the night without looking back.

# Chapter 6

Danny woke up the next morning stark naked, curled up in a doorway. The old woman who lived there got quite a surprise when she went to sweep her step. Danny got quite a surprise, too, when she nearly bashed his head in with the broom.

"You're lucky I don't call the police," she called after him, as he made his getaway.

He took shelter behind some wheelie bins in an alley. The memories from the night before came flooding back. He remembered hunting rabbits, the blood trickling down his throat and the heavy smell of raw meat. Those poor creatures. He felt hot bile rise in his throat, the urge to vomit.

He knew what he had become, something he thought only existed in legends and fairy tales. The animal that attacked him yesterday was no ordinary wolf.

But what now? How was he going to hide this from Mum? His mind raced with unanswered questions. There was so much he didn't understand.

But, first things first, he needed clothes.

He hopped over a fence and pinched the first things he could grab from a washing line. When he arrived home he was expecting an earful, but instead Mum threw her arms around him. She didn't even seem to notice that he was wearing skin-tight jeans and a jumper that was three sizes too big.

"Thank God you're okay. I was so worried it was you."

Danny had his excuse ready. "I'm sorry, I just went to my mate's and …" He stopped as her words sank in. "You were worried *what* was me?"

"Haven't you heard?"

She guided him into the living room and pointed at the television. Danny read the rolling headline: "Man killed by wild animal." Next, a picture of the victim appeared on the screen. Danny's eyes widened. It was a face he recognised: the man he had attacked last night.

The reporter's voice droned on. "The victim was killed in the early hours of this morning. The body was covered in bite and scratch marks believed to be the work of a large animal, perhaps a rabid dog. Police believe the animal may also be responsible for the string of recent disappearances."

It didn't make sense. Danny had stopped himself. He'd left the man unharmed.

There was only one thing that could have killed him like that – a werewolf. If it wasn't Danny, then it must have been the same wolf that had attacked him.

Danny needed answers. He ran upstairs.

"*Daniel*," Mum called after him. He hated it when she called him that. "We need to talk."

"Later," he shouted, slamming his door shut behind him. How was he supposed to explain this to Mum? He couldn't even explain it to himself.

"Fine." He heard Mum's muffled voice from downstairs. "I'm going shopping, *then* we're going to talk."

# Chapter 7

Danny heard the front door shut as Mum left. Good. That would give him some time to figure this out, but he would have to be quick.

He opened his laptop and his fingers rattled on the keys. He looked up "werewolf" and refreshed his memory. His eyes darted over the information on screen: "The change is often associated with the appearance of the full moon." Next he entered "lunar calendar" into the search bar. He frowned. Last night wasn't a full moon. Something else must have triggered the change, but what?

He locked his bedroom door and stood in front of the mirror, pale and skinny. He made his fingers like claws and bared his teeth.

"Change," he said. Nothing happened. "Transform." Still nothing. "Wolf ... Hairy?"

He was clutching at straws. There was no magic password. The change had come from within. He remembered the way it rose up from his stomach and consumed his whole body.

He tried to remember what he was thinking when he changed, what he was feeling. His mind was blank.

He sat back down at his laptop and stared blankly at what was on the screen. Myths and fairy tales. Stories. None of it was going to help. What was happening to him was real.

Danny heard the front door. Mum was home. He gave up. Even if he did work out how to change, he couldn't risk it with her here.

After a short while, Mum called from downstairs. "Tea's ready."

He closed his laptop. He would have to figure it out later.

# Chapter 8

Mum was waiting for him at the table.

Even in human form, Danny could feel the hunger rumbling quietly. It was getting stronger. He sniffed the kitchen air, hoping for the smell of steak or some other meat.

"What are we having?"

"Salad," Mum said.

Danny rolled his eyes. Great.

Danny sat down and pushed the plate away. "I'm not hungry."

Mum sighed. "Danny, you've been acting really strange lately. I'm worried about you. Is something wrong?"

Danny shook his head.

"Oh, really? Have you looked in the mirror lately?"

He glanced at the mirror in the hall, worried about what he might see. The bruise where Carver hit him had got worse and a purple swelling marked the beginnings of a black eye.

"I know you didn't *fall* over," Mum continued. "Are you being bullied?"

"No."

"Come on, I know what the lads round here are like."

"No," Danny repeated. He was getting frustrated. He had bigger things to worry about.

Mum sighed. "Don't let those idiots walk all over you. They think they can do whatever they want. My friend Margaret was telling me that just this morning she saw that Carver boy streaking through town. Can you believe that?"

Danny tensed. "He was naked?"

Mum kept talking, but her voice seemed far away. Danny's mind raced. He remembered his own clothes tearing when he had changed into the wolf. It all added up. Carver had chased him into the woods right before he was attacked by the wolf. It was no coincidence. It was Carver who attacked him. Carver was the werewolf.

"Are you listening to me, Daniel?" Mum said.

He wasn't. He was wondering if he should try to find Carver and confront him. As it turned out, he didn't have to.

# Chapter 9

The sound of breaking glass made Danny start.
A brick came through the window and clattered
onto the table. Mum screamed as tiny shards of
glass scattered across the floor.

A note was wrapped around the brick. Danny
read it.

*Little pig, little pig, let me come in.*

The front door rattled. Fingers reached in and
flicked open the letterbox. A pair of eyes appeared
in the slot.

"Come out, come out wherever you are."

Danny recognised the voice. "Carver."

"I knew you were being bullied," Mum said. "I'll be damned if I'm being terrorised in my own house by these hoodlums. I'm phoning the police."

"I wouldn't do that if I were you," Carver hissed through the letterbox. "Or I'll huff and I'll puff and I'll blow this door down."

"Stop!" Danny warned. Mum had half-lifted the phone and the dial tone droned. "Don't phone the police. He'll kill us before they get here."

Mum frowned. "Kill us? Danny, he's just a boy!"

But Carver wasn't just a boy.

"If I come with you, will you leave her alone?" Danny said.

"Scout's honour." Carver winked.

Danny opened the door. Carver grinned. A penknife gleamed in his hand.

"What on earth are you doing?" Mum cried. She tried to go after them, but Carver held up the knife and snarled. The knife didn't scare her. The snarl did. It wasn't like any sound a human could make. She stopped and clasped a shaking hand over her mouth.

"I'm sorry," Danny said, and closed the door.

# Chapter 10

Carver swung his arm around Danny. To a passer-by they might have looked like friends, but Danny felt the knife prodding the flesh of his back.

"Walk," Carver ordered.

"Where are you taking me?"

"The same place I should have got you the first time, if it wasn't for that dirty trick," Carver said. He patted Danny's pockets. No pepper spray. "Nothing to save you this time."

Carver wasn't the type to make empty threats, and Danny knew it. He needed the wolf. It was his only chance. But he still didn't know how to change. He tried to remember what had triggered it last time, but the memory escaped him. His best hope for now was to keep Carver talking.

"How did you become this way?" Danny asked.

"The same way you did." Carver sensed Danny's confusion and chuckled. "What? Did you think I was the only one?"

Danny gulped. "Everyone who's been going missing. You killed them all, didn't you?"

"Of course I did. Human blood is the only thing that can really feed the hunger. But you'd know that, wouldn't you?"

Danny remembered hunting rabbits in the woods. How they were just appetisers. How his killer instincts had pulled him into the city to look for the main course. "I'm not like you," he snapped.

Carver snorted. "Because you pulled yourself away from that guy in the suit the other night? Just because you stopped yourself once doesn't mean you can do it again. The hunger is too strong."

Danny tensed. "You were there?"

"I followed you. I couldn't let you blow my cover. But then you let him go. I had to kill him before he told anyone what he'd seen. Before I could drag his body to the woods, a car drove past. I had to leave him. Now everyone's talking, and it's all your fault." Carver pushed the knife harder against Danny's back. "But if I get rid of you, this will all blow over soon enough."

The slap of shoes against pavement became the crunch of leaves as they left the path and entered the woods. Danny was running out of time.

"My mum will phone the police. She'll tell them about you coming to our house. That stunt with the brick? Way to draw attention to yourself. They'll know it was you."

Carver laughed. "No, they won't. You're the only one who knows my dirty, hairy little secret. They'll find you *all chewed up*. They think the killer is a wild animal, remember? But I'm just a boy. That's what your mum said, isn't it? Even if she suspects any different, they'll think she's crazy."

Carver stopped in a little clearing not too far from the town.

"This should do it." Carver smiled. His teeth were already sharpening into fangs. His voice became a growl. "Go ahead and run. I'll catch you."

Danny shook his head. "I'm not running this time."

# Chapter 11

Danny stayed rooted to the spot. He balled his hands into fists to stop them shaking. He didn't want Carver to see his fear. He remembered the last time they clashed. The sting of humiliation was still sore. Danny's breathing became heavy. His whole body tensed. He could feel the blood-lust building.

Then he realised. Anger. That was the trigger. That was the key to unlocking the wolf.

The animal roared to be set free. This time Danny didn't fight it. He was going to need it.

His skin prickled as hairs sprouted all over his body. Fangs and claws ripped free. He heard the tear of his clothes as his muscles ballooned.

He looked at Carver. Their eyes locked. Wolf against wolf.

Carver snarled. His breath steamed in the frosty air. His muzzle wrinkled back over a row of needle-like teeth.

Danny reared up on his hind legs, snorting. He wasn't afraid. He'd been afraid for too long. A growl rumbled in his throat. *Come and get me.*

Carver charged towards him. His paws hammered the ground. Danny met him head-on. They clashed in a frenzy of ripping claws. Danny twisted his neck. He was trying to get a grip on Carver's fur, but his opponent was too quick and agile. The air filled with the sound of snarls and snorts and snapping teeth.

Just as Danny found a place to fix his jaws, Carver's paw flashed across his face. An arc of blood splattered the surroundings. The pain was sharp, like burning.

Carver pounced and Danny felt the wind knocked out of him. His back hit the hard ground. He felt the weight of Carver's massive paws holding him down. Carver bared his fangs and roared. Danny felt the hot breath on his face. Those vice-like jaws hovered over his neck, waiting to clamp shut at any moment.

The strength was being crushed out of him, but Danny saw his chance. His front paws were pinned, but his two hind paws were free.

He pressed them against Carver's chest and kicked out with all the strength he had left. Carver whined as he was launched through the air. He hit the ground with a thud.

Danny quickly pinned him down. Their eyes met for a moment. Danny didn't see any human in them. All he saw was a monster.

He bit.

# Chapter 12

For a moment Danny stood perched on his hind legs. He closed his eyes and breathed. It was over.

Danny felt himself changing. His claws disappeared into the tips of blood-stained hands. His hairs shrank back into smooth, pale skin. When he looked at the still body at his feet, Carver was no longer a wolf. He was a boy, covered in blood.

Danny heard shouting. He looked back towards town. Blue lights flashed between the bars of the trees. Doors slammed. Dogs barked. Mum must have phoned the police and they'd come looking for him.

Danny froze. The police were about to find him standing over Carver's dead body. He wouldn't be able to explain. They'd put two and two together and get five. They'd think Danny was the killer all along.

The beam of a flashlight blinded him. A voice shouted, "I've found him."

Danny only had a few moments to make a decision. He bolted into the forest, running as fast as he could.

He didn't want to run, but he had no choice. He knew Mum would worry. He knew how much she'd miss him, how much his leaving would hurt her. He'd miss her too, but he couldn't return, not unless he could figure out some way to clear his name.

He glanced back over his shoulder. One last look at the life he was leaving behind.

In the meantime, he had a mission. There were more of these things out there, killing people. He would stop them. He would hunt the hunters. But it wasn't a mission he could share with anyone. He remembered Carver's warning: *Just because you stopped yourself once doesn't mean you can do it again. The hunger is too strong.*

Danny couldn't risk getting close to anyone. If he lost his temper, even for a second, he could end up hurting someone.

He had no choice.

He would have to do it alone.

He was a lone wolf.

# Reader challenge

## Word hunt

 On page 16, find an adjective that means "tangled".

 On page 27, find an adjective that means "to do with the moon".

 On page 44, find words that describe the noises the werewolves made.

## Story sense

 What are the first clues that Danny is becoming a werewolf?

 How do you think Danny felt when he nearly killed the man in the suit?

 Why did his mum think Danny was being bullied?

 Why did Danny choose to stay and fight Carver rather than running away again?

 How did Danny win the fight in the end?

# Your views

**9** What did you think of the way the author uses words to describe the fight between Danny and Carver (pages 44 to 47)?

**10** What do you think Danny will do next? Give reasons.

# Spell it

With a partner, look at these words and then cover them up.

- cried
- weird
- pierce

Take it in turns for one of you to read the words aloud. The other person has to try and spell each word. Check your answers, then swap over.

# Try it

With a partner, imagine you are acting out part of the story. Make a freeze-frame of the fight between the two werewolves. Look at page 44 to get ideas.

William Collins's dream of knowledge for all began with the publication of his first book in 1819. A self-educated mill worker, he not only enriched millions of lives, but also founded a flourishing publishing house. Today, staying true to this spirit, Collins books are packed with inspiration, innovation and practical expertise. They place you at the centre of a world of possibility and give you exactly what you need to explore it.

Collins. Freedom to teach.

Published by Collins Education
An imprint of HarperCollins*Publishers*
77–85 Fulham Palace Road
Hammersmith
London
W6 8JB

Browse the complete Collins Education catalogue at **www.collinseducation.com**

Text by Alan Gibbons and Robbie Gibbons © HarperCollins*Publishers* 2012
Illustrations by Matt Timson © HarperCollins*Publishers* 2012

Series consultants: Alan Gibbons and Natalie Packer

10 9 8 7 6 5 4 3 2 1
ISBN 978-0-00-746486-9

British Library Cataloguing in Publication Data.
A catalogue record for this publication is available from the British Library.

Commissioned by Catherine Martin
Edited and project-managed by Sue Chapple
Illustration management by Tim Satterthwaite
Picture research by Grace Glendinning
Design and typesetting by Jordan Publishing Design Limited
Cover design by Paul Manning

### Acknowledgements

The publishers would like to thank the students and teachers of the following schools for their help in trialling the Read On series:

Southfields Academy, London
Queensbury School, Queensbury, Bradford
Langham C of E Primary School, Langham, Rutland
Ratton School, Eastbourne, East Sussex
Northfleet School for Girls, North Fleet, Kent
Westergate Community School, Chichester, West Sussex
Bottesford C of E Primary School, Bottesford, Nottinghamshire
Woodfield Academy, Redditch, Worcestershire
St Richard's Catholic College, Bexhill, East Sussex